In
Abigail's Garden

In
Abigail's Garden

Compiled and illustrated by Helen Williams

E. P. Dutton   New York

For Chris and Abi and Bella and Rosie and Tess, Helen Williams

"The Land" by Vita Sackville-West is reproduced here in part
by kind permission of William Heinemann Ltd.

"The Wood of Flowers" by James Stevens is reproduced here
by kind permission of Macmillan Publishing Company, New York.

Copyright for this anthology © 1986 Methuen Children's Books Ltd
Illustrations copyright © 1986 Helen Williams

This anthology first published in the United States in 1987
by E. P. Dutton, 2 Park Avenue, New York, N.Y. 10016

Originally published in Great Britain in 1986
by Methuen Children's Books Ltd,
11 New Fetter Lane, London EC4P 4EE

Printed in Hong Kong by South China Printing Co.

OBE   First Edition
ISBN: 0-525-44281-2   10 9 8 7 6 5 4 3 2 1

The kiss of the sun for pardon
The song of the birds for mirth
You are nearer God's heart in a garden
Than anywhere else on Earth.

Pull the primrose, sister Anne!
Pull as many as you can.
– Here are daisies, take your fill;
Pansies, and the cuckoo-flower:
Of the lofty daffodil
Make your bed, or make your bower;
Fill your lap and fill your bosom;
Only spare the strawberry-blossom!

Primroses, the Spring may love them –
Summer knows but little of them:
Violets, a barren kind,
Withered on the ground must lie;
Daisies leave no fruit behind
When the pretty flowerets die;
Pluck them, and another year
As many will be blowing here.

God has given a kindlier power
To the favoured strawberry-flower.
Hither soon as Spring is fled
You and Charles and I will walk;
Lurking berries, ripe and red,
Then will hang on every stalk,
Each within its leafy bower;
And for that promise spare the flower!

from Children Gathering Flowers WILLIAM WORDSWORTH

I went to the wood of flowers
(No-one was with me)
I was there alone for hours
I was happy as could be
In the wood of flowers
There was grass on the ground
There were buds on the tree
And the wind had a sound
Of such gaiety
That I was as happy
As happy could be,
In the wood of flowers

The Wood of Flowers JAMES STEVENS

There once the walls
Of the ruined cottage stood.
The periwinkle crawls
With flowers in its hair into the wood.

In flowerless hours
Never will the bank fail,
With everlasting flowers
On fragments of blue plates, to tell the tale.

A Tale EDWARD THOMAS

I remember, I remember,
The roses, red and white,
The violets, and the lily-cups,
Those flowers made of light!
The lilacs where the robin built,
And where my brother set
The laburnum on his birthday, –
The tree is living yet!

from I Remember, I Remember THOMAS HOOD

The Cliff-top has a carpet
Of lilac, gold and green:
The blue sky bounds the ocean,
The white clouds sail between.

A flock of gulls are wheeling
And wailing round my seat;
Above my head the heaven,
The sea beneath my feet.

The Cliff-Top ROBERT BRIDGES

I know a bank whereon the wild thyme blows,
Where oxlips and the nodding violet grows
Quite overcanopied with luscious woodbine,

With sweet musk-roses and with eglantine:
There sleeps Titania, some time of the night,
Lull'd in these flowers with dances and delight....

from A Midsummer Night's Dream WILLIAM SHAKESPEARE

But for this summer's quick delight
Sow marigold, and sow the bright
Frail poppy that with noonday dies
But wakens to a fresh surprise;
Along the pathway stones be set
Sweet Alysson and mignonette,
That when the full midsummer's come
On scented clumps the bees may hum . . .

. . . Nor be the little space forgot
For herbs to spice the kitchen pot:
Mint, pennyroyal, bergamot,
Tarragon and melilot,
Dill for witchcraft, prisoners' rue,
Coriander, costmary,
Tansy, thyme, Sweet Cicely,
Saffron, balm, and rosemary . . .

from The Land VITA SACKVILLE-WEST

What wondrous life is this I lead!
Ripe apples drop about my head;
The luscious clusters of the vine
Upon my mouth do crush their wine;
The nectarine and curious peach
Into my hands themselves do reach;
Stumbling on melons, as I pass,
Ensnared with flowers, I fall on grass.

How well the skilful gardener drew
Of flowers and herbs this dial new!
Where, from above, the milder sun
Does through a fragrant zodiac run:
And, as it works, the industrious bee
Computes its time as well as we.
How could such sweet and wholesome hours
Be reckoned, but with herbs and flowers.

from The Garden ANDREW MARVELL

I mind me in the days departed
How often underneath the sun
With childish bounds I used to run
To a garden long deserted

The trees were interwoven wild
And spread their boughs enough about
To keep both sheep and shepherd out
But not a happy child

Adventurous joy it was for me
I crept beneath the boughs and found
A circle smooth of mossy ground
Beneath the poplar tree.

from The Deserted Garden ELIZABETH B BROWNING

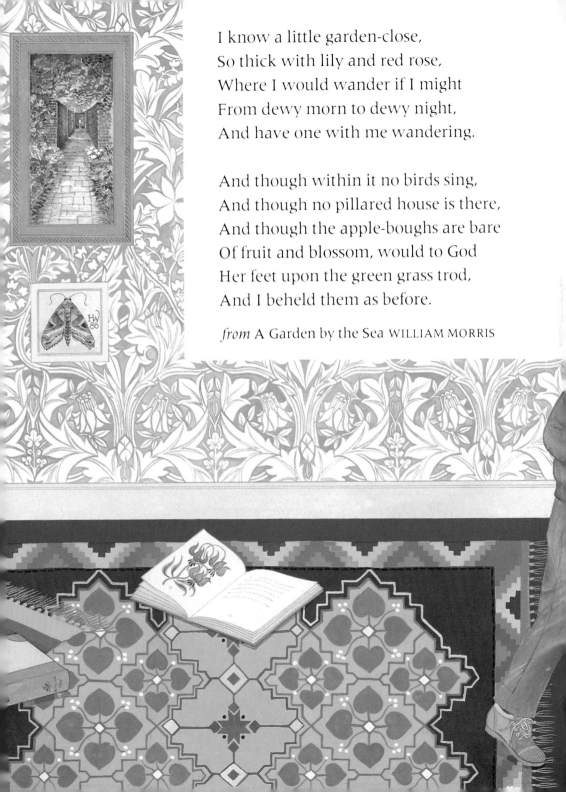

I know a little garden-close,
So thick with lily and red rose,
Where I would wander if I might
From dewy morn to dewy night,
And have one with me wandering.

And though within it no birds sing,
And though no pillared house is there,
And though the apple-boughs are bare
Of fruit and blossom, would to God
Her feet upon the green grass trod,
And I beheld them as before.

from A Garden by the Sea WILLIAM MORRIS

In the other gardens
    And all up the vale,
From the autumn bonfires
    See the smoke trail!

Pleasant Summer over
    And all the summer flowers,
The red fire blazes,
    The grey smoke towers.

Sing a song of seasons!
    Something bright in all!
Flowers in the Summer,
    Fires in the Fall!

Autumn Fires ROBERT LOUIS STEVENSON

When the golden day is done,
    Through the closing portal,
Child and garden, flower and sun,
    Vanish all things mortal. . .

        . . . There my garden grows again
           Green and rosy painted,
        As at eve behind the pane
           From my eyes it fainted.

Just as it was shut away,
    Toy-like, in the even,
Here I see it glow with day
    Under glowing heaven.

        Every path and every plot,
           Every bush of roses,
        Every blue forget-me-not
           Where the dew reposes.

from Night and Day ROBERT LOUIS STEVENSON